But sometimes,
Hector got cross
with Hummingbird.

Whenever Hector just wanted
a nice, quiet snack,

Hummingbird wouldn't stop talking . . .

Hey, Hector!
Is that a custard apple?

I love custard apples!
I'm going to eat this one!
Oh, no! I'm going to eat that one!

Shall I eat your one?
Hector?
Hec-torrr!

And whenever Hector wanted a nice, quiet scratch on a tree,

Hummingbird wouldn't stop copying him . . .

Hey, Hector!
Are you scratching?
I'm going to scratch, too!

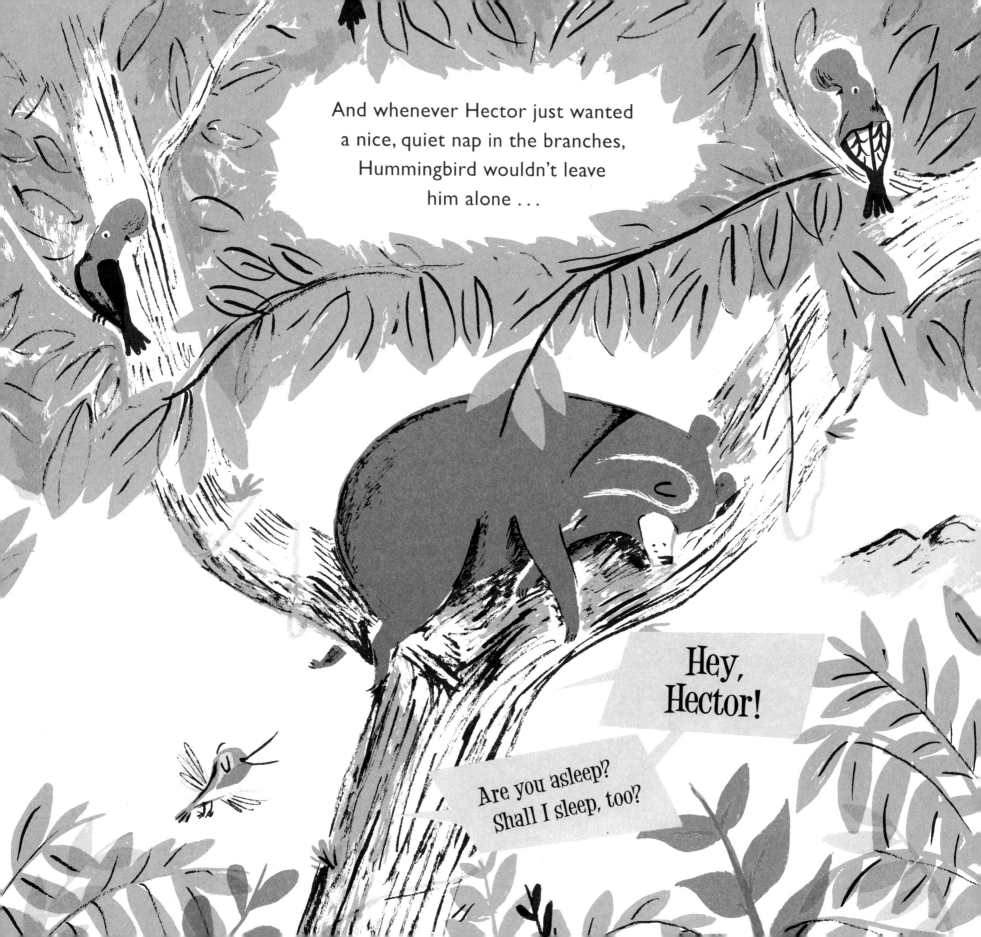

And whenever Hector just wanted a nice, quiet nap in the branches, Hummingbird wouldn't leave him alone . . .

Hey, Hector!

Are you asleep? Shall I sleep, too?

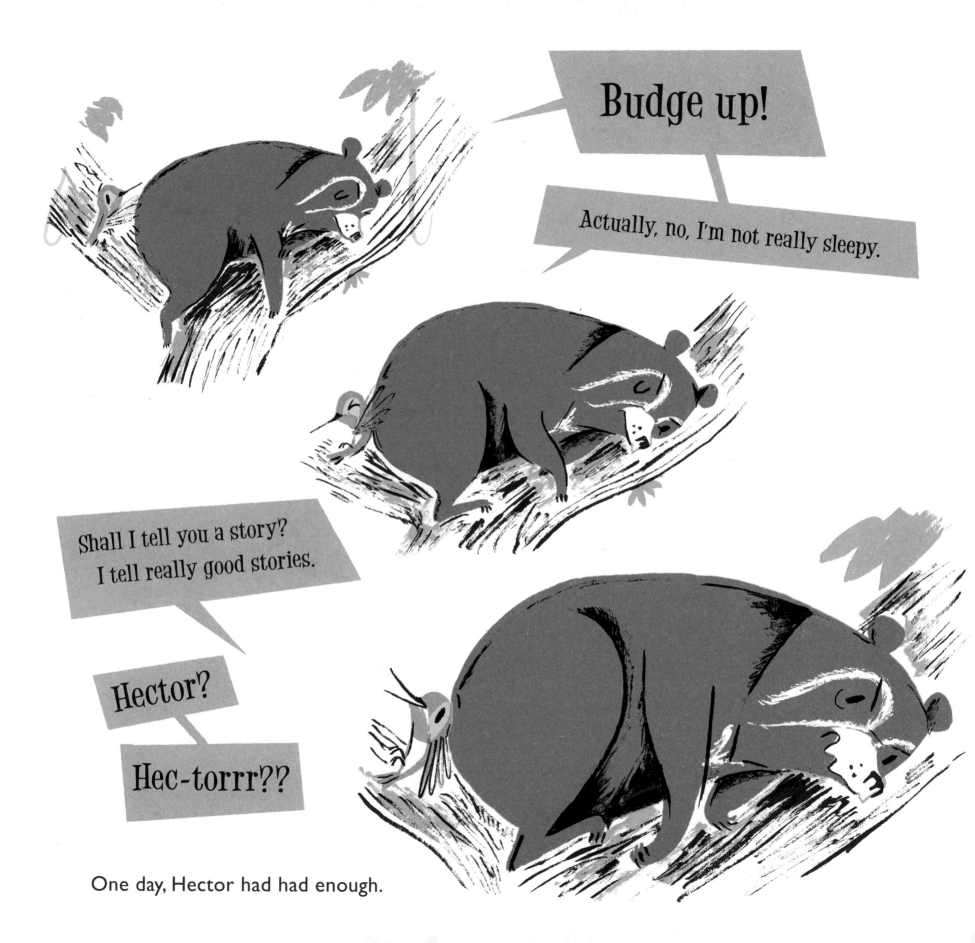

One day, Hector had had enough.

"ARRGH!!"

cried Hector.

"Leave me alone!"

Hector stomped off into the jungle.
"I'm going to find a bit of peace and quiet!"

Hummingbird was sad. He'd never known
Hector was cross with him.

He decided he'd better follow and find out why.

Hey, Hector!

What's peace and quiet?

Is it in the jungle?
Can I help you look for it?

"Stop following me!" said Hector.
"I want to be on my own!"

So Hummingbird
stopped following him.

Mostly.

Hector walked deep
into the jungle.

At last he was on his own.
He felt very excited.

But a little bit odd.

Maybe he was
just hungry.

So Hector picked a custard apple,
and sat down to have a nice, quiet snack.

The fruit was sweet.
And delicious.

But it felt funny eating it on his own. "Hummingbird would really like this custard apple," thought Hector.

Next, Hector found what looked like the scratchiest tree in the jungle. He settled down to have a nice, quiet scratch.

But it felt funny scratching on his own.

"Hummingbird would love scratching on this tree," sighed Hector.

Dark fell, and Hector settled down for a nap.
The jungle was noisy at night, and a little bit scary.
Hector couldn't sleep.

SQUEAK!

EEK!

"I wish Hummingbird was here," sniffed Hector. "He could tell me a story."

"Hummingbird!" cried Hector.
"You're here! I missed you!"

I missed you, too!

Except I was here all along.

"Here all along?" said Hector.
"I thought I told you not to follow me!"

But, why?

"Because you never stop talking!"

I'm just being friendly.

"And you're always copying me!"

You always have really good ideas.

"Oh," said Hector. "Really?"

Just then, Hector had his best idea yet.

"Hummingbird, can you copy me now, by being really, really quiet?"

And he did.
Mostly.

How many of these animals did you spot in the jungle?

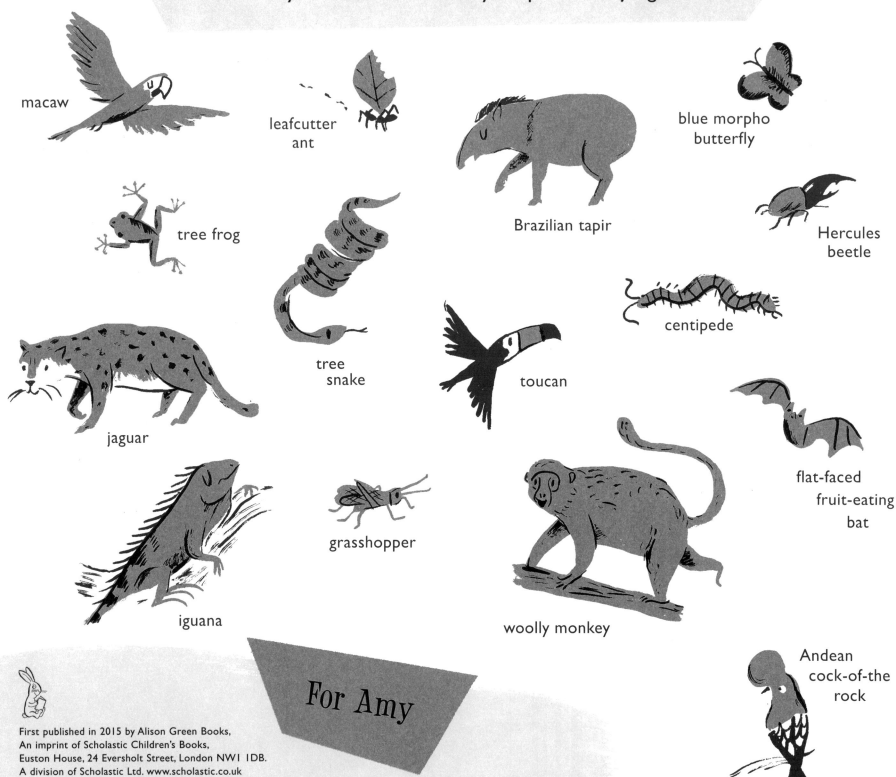

macaw

leafcutter ant

Brazilian tapir

blue morpho butterfly

tree frog

Hercules beetle

tree snake

centipede

jaguar

toucan

flat-faced fruit-eating bat

iguana

grasshopper

woolly monkey

Andean cock-of-the rock

For Amy

First published in 2015 by Alison Green Books,
An imprint of Scholastic Children's Books,
Euston House, 24 Eversholt Street, London NW1 1DB.
A division of Scholastic Ltd. www.scholastic.co.uk
Text & Illustrations copyright © 2015 Nicholas John Frith
HB ISBN: 978 1 407146 40 9 • PB ISBN: 978 1 407146 41 6